All I Am

by Eileen Roe

illustrated by Helen Cogancherry

Bradbury Press   New York

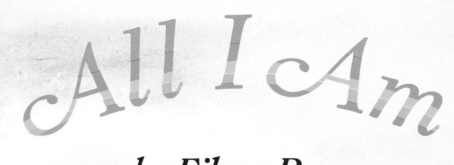

I am a child.

I am a friend.

I am a neighbor.

I am a helper.

I am a listener and a thinker.

I am an artist.

I am an animal lover.

I am a singer.

I am a dancer.

Some days I am a daydreamer,
wondering about all I am.

Some nights I am a stargazer,
wondering about all I will be.

For Jack — E.R.

To Jason, my little stargazer, for all you are and wondering about all you will be — H.C.

Text copyright © 1990 by Eileen Roe. Illustrations copyright © 1990 by Helen Cogancherry.

Library of Congress Cataloging-in-Publication Data   Roe, Eileen.   All I am.   Summary: A child is a friend, neighbor, helper, painter, dancer, daydreamer, and stargazer.   [1. Identity—Fiction.   2. Self-perception—Fiction]
I. Cogancherry, Helen, ill.   II. Title.   PZ7.R62A1   1990   [E]   88-30510
ISBN 0-02-777372-8